Susie Gubik

Mom
April '17

Get Up, Rick!

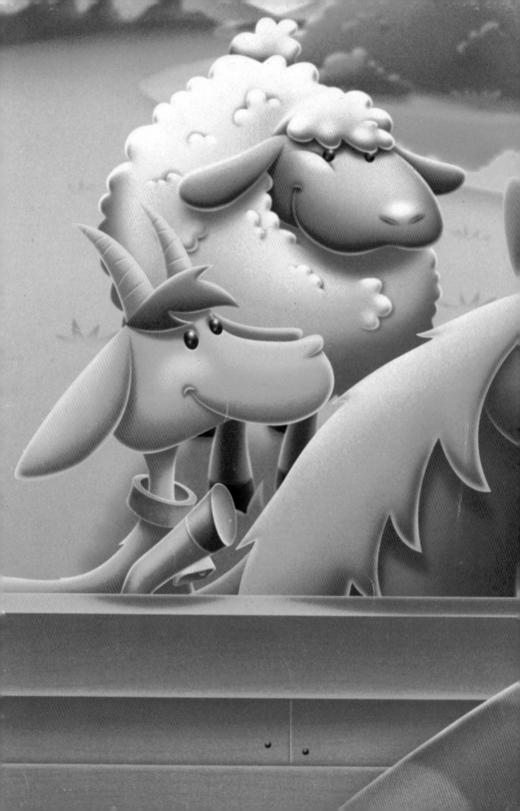

Get Up, Rick!

F. Isabel Campoy

Illustrated by
Bernard Adnet

Green Light Readers
Harcourt, Inc.

Orlando   Austin   New York
San Diego   Toronto   London

Oh, no! It is late.

Where is Rick?

Is Rick sick?

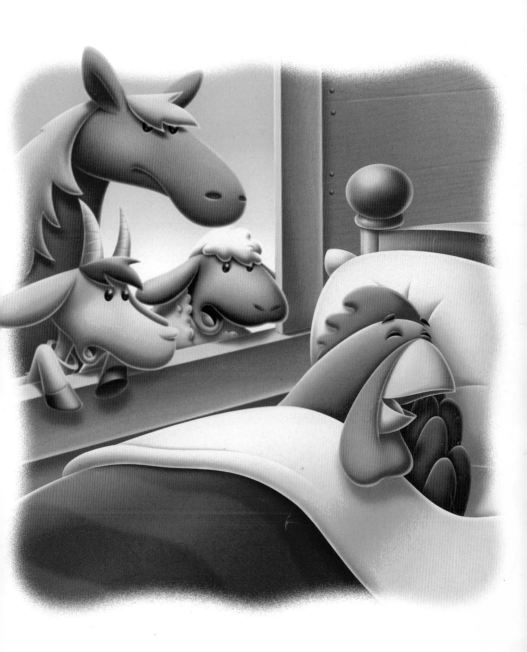

No! Rick is fast asleep!

Get up, Rick! It is late!

Cock-a-doodle-doo!

Oh, Rick, it is too late.

Now Rick is sad.

We will help Rick.

We will get him a gift.

What is in the sack?

Will it help Rick?

Yes!

Cock-a-doodle-doo!

Response Activity

In this story, the animals talk. What would we hear if we could understand what animals say? Make a page for a class book about what the animals are saying.

- Choose an animal.
- Think about what it might say.
- Draw and write about what your animal says.

It's snack time!

Let's go to the park! Please! Please!

Share your page with your classmates. Put the pages together to make a class book.

Meet the Author

F. Isabel Campoy

F. Isabel Campoy lives on a ranch part of the year. A rooster wakes her up every morning. "He doesn't have an alarm clock, either!" she says. "I wanted to imagine the opposite situation, and so I wrote about Rick."

Meet the Illustrator
Bernard Adnet

Bernard Adnet grew up in France. As a child,
he spent many hours alone drawing, but he also
drew for his nieces and nephews.
Today, he still makes children
happy with his drawings.

Requests for permission to make copies of any part of the work should be submitted online
at www.harcourt.com/contact or mailed to the following address: Permissions Department,
Harcourt, Inc., 6277 Sea Harbor Drive, Orlando, Florida 32887-6777.

www.HarcourtBooks.com

First Green Light Readers edition 2007

Green Light Readers is a trademark of Harcourt, Inc., registered in the
United States of America and/or other jurisdictions.

Library of Congress Cataloging-in-Publication Data
Campoy, F. Isabel.
Get up, Rick!/F. Isabel Campoy; illustrated by Bernard Adnet.
p. cm.
"Green Light Readers."
Summary: When Rick the rooster sleeps through the
sunrise, his clever friends give him just the thing to help.
[1. Roosters—Fiction.] I. Adnet, Bernard, ill. II. Title.
PZ7.C16153Ge 2007
[E]—dc22   2006035418
ISBN 978-0-15-206266-8
ISBN 978-0-15-206272-9 (pb)

A C E G H F D B
A C E G H F D B (pb)

Ages 4-6
Grade: I
Guided Reading Level: C
Reading Recovery Level: 4

Green Light Readers
For the reader who's ready to GO!

"A must-have for any family with a beginning reader."—*Boston Sunday Herald*

"You can't go wrong with adding several copies of these terrific books to your beginning-to-read collection."—*School Library Journal*

"A winner for the beginner."—*Booklist*

Five Tips to Help Your Child Become a Great Reader

1. Get involved. Reading aloud to and with your child is just as important as encouraging your child to read independently.

2. Be curious. Ask questions about what your child is reading.

3. Make reading fun. Allow your child to pick books on subjects that interest her or him.

4. Words are everywhere—not just in books. Practice reading signs, packages, and cereal boxes with your child.

5. Set a good example. Make sure your child sees YOU reading.

Why Green Light Readers Is the Best Series for Your New Reader

• Created exclusively for beginning readers by some of the biggest and brightest names in children's books

• Reinforces the reading skills your child is learning in school

• Encourages children to read—and finish—books by themselves

• Offers extra enrichment through fun, age-appropriate activities unique to each story

• Incorporates characteristics of the Reading Recovery program used by educators

• Developed with Harcourt School Publishers and credentialed educational consultants

Daniel's Pet
Alma Flor Ada/G. Brian Karas

Sometimes
Keith Baker

A New Home
Tim Bowers

A Big Surprise
Kristi T. Butler/Pamela Paparone

Rip's Secret Spot
Kristi T. Butler/Joe Cepeda

Get Up, Rick!
F. Isabel Campoy/Bernard Adnet

Sid's Surprise
Candace Carter/Joung Un Kim

Cloudy Day Sunny Day
Donald Crews

Jan Has a Doll
Janice Earl/Tricia Tusa

Rabbit and Turtle Go to School
Lucy Floyd/Christopher Denise

The Tapping Tale
Judy Giglio/Joe Cepeda

The Big, Big Wall
Reginald Howard/Ariane Dewey/Jose Aruego

Sam and the Bag
Alison Jeffries/Dan Andreasen

The Hat
Holly Keller

Down on the Farm
Rita Lascaro

Just Clowning Around: Two Stories
Steven MacDonald/David McPhail

Big Brown Bear
David McPhail

Big Pig and Little Pig
David McPhail

Jack and Rick
David McPhail

Rick Is Sick
David McPhail

Best Friends
Anna Michaels/G. Brian Karas

Come Here, Tiger!
Alex Moran/Lisa Campbell Ernst

Lost!
Alex Moran/Daniel Moreton

Popcorn
Alex Moran/Betsy Everitt

Sam and Jack: Three Stories
Alex Moran/Tim Bowers

Six Silly Foxes
Alex Moran/Keith Baker

What Day Is It?
Alex Moran/Daniel Moreton

Todd's Box
Paula Sullivan/Nadine Bernard Westcott

The Picnic
David K. Williams/Laura Ovresat

Tick Tock
David K. Williams/Laura Ovresat

Look for more Green Light Readers wherever books are sold!